SO-AJG-406

The Little Knight Who Battled a Dragon

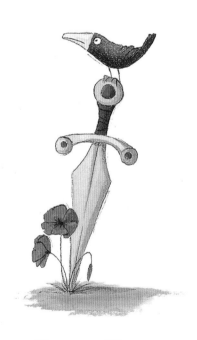

GILLES TIBO
GENEVIÈVE DESPRÉS

Scholastic Canada Ltd.
Toronto New York London Auckland Sydney
Mexico City New Delhi Hong Kong Buenos Aires

Scholastic Canada Ltd.
604 King Street West, Toronto, Ontario M5V 1E1, Canada

Scholastic Inc.
557 Broadway, New York, NY 10012, USA

Scholastic Australia Pty Limited
PO Box 579, Gosford, NSW 2250, Australia

Scholastic New Zealand Limited
Private Bag 94407, Botany, Manukau 2163, New Zealand

Scholastic Children's Books
Euston House, 24 Eversholt Street, London NW1 1DB, UK

www.scholastic.ca

Library and Archives Canada Cataloguing in Publication
Tibo, Gilles, 1951-
[Petit chevalier qui affrontait les dragons. English]
The little knight who battled a dragon / Gilles Tibo ; illustrated by
Geneviève Després ; translated by Petra Johannson.
(The little knight)
Translation of: Le petit chevalier qui affrontait les dragons.
ISBN 978-1-4431-4861-0 (paperback)
I. Després, Geneviève, illustrator II. Johannson, Petra, translator
III. Title. IV. Title: Petit chevalier qui affrontait les dragons. English.

PS8589.I26P42513 2016   jC843'.54   C2016-901222-0

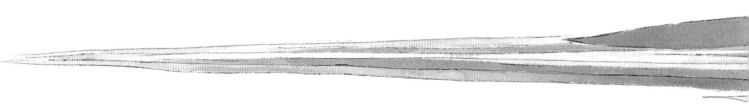

Text copyright © 2017 by Gilles Tibo.
Illustrations copyright © 2017 by Geneviève Després.
All rights reserved.
No part of this publication may be reproduced or stored in a retrieval system, or
transmitted in any form or by any means, electronic, mechanical, recording, or
otherwise, without written permission of the publisher, Scholastic Canada Ltd.,
604 King Street West, Toronto, Ontario M5V 1E1, Canada. In the case of photocopying
or other reprographic copying, a licence must be obtained from Access Copyright
(Canadian Copyright Licensing Agency), 56 Wellesley Street West, Suite 320,
Toronto, Ontario M5S 2S3 (1-800-893-5777).

6 5 4 3 2 1   Printed in Malaysia 108   17 18 19 20 21

To my son Simon, tamer of dragons.
— GILLES TIBO

For Philippe.
— GENEVIÈVE DESPRÉS

A hammock hanging between two towers.

Bats dance around the moon.

Knightly pyjamas.

A mouse hides in the hammock.

A supply of chocolate cake.

Bartlett dreams that she is chasing a mouse.

Once upon a time there was a little knight whose life was very easy. During the day, he had fun training flies. At night, he relaxed in a hammock, making friends with the bats.

But one evening, the earth and the sky started to shake. BOOOM! BOOOM! BOOOOOOOOM! The bats flew away. The moon and stars faded. With a flash of heat, a giant flame rose up from the other side of the forest.

Pipe that can be used for emergencies.

A few minutes later, the doors of the little knight's fortress also started to shake. BOOOM! BOOOM! BOOOOOOOOM! The little knight jumped off his hammock, slid down a long pipe, landed on a feather bed, rushed to the fortress doors and threw them open.

Mr. Baxter trembles with fear.

Mrs. Singer trembles with fear.

The blacksmith's moustache trembles with fear.

The Balko twins tremble with fear.

Ms Kitty's glasses tremble with fear.

The witc
tremble
with fea

The terrified villagers were all yelling at the same time: "Help! I keep hearing BOOM! BOOM! Help! There are giant flames in the sky! Help! Enemies are after us! Help! They will burn down the forest!"

Miss Chance trembles with fear.

George Forester trembles with fear.

Mr. Singer trembles with fear.

The Singer triplets tremble with fear.

The little knight looked at the flames in the sky and sighed.

"All I have is a wooden sword, a wooden shield and a wooden horse. I can't battle a fire with those!"

The villagers looked at each other in surprise. Then Mrs. Singer said, "We'll be right back!"

And with that, everyone ran off.

All the birds
fly away.

The little knight is barefoot
and still not fully awake.

Non-fireproof pyjamas.

Whose shoe
is this?

Someone has
lost a shoe.

Whose gloves
are these?

All the cats run away.

Bartlett jumps at each BOOOM! BOOOM!

Fireproof iron horse who loves chocolate.

The sky lit up once more. The earth trembled again. BOOOM! BOOOM! BOOOOOOOOM!

The villagers returned with everything needed to fight the flames: a metal shield, a steel lasso, a flame-proof breastplate and a very old iron horse, which had belonged to the blacksmith's grandfather.

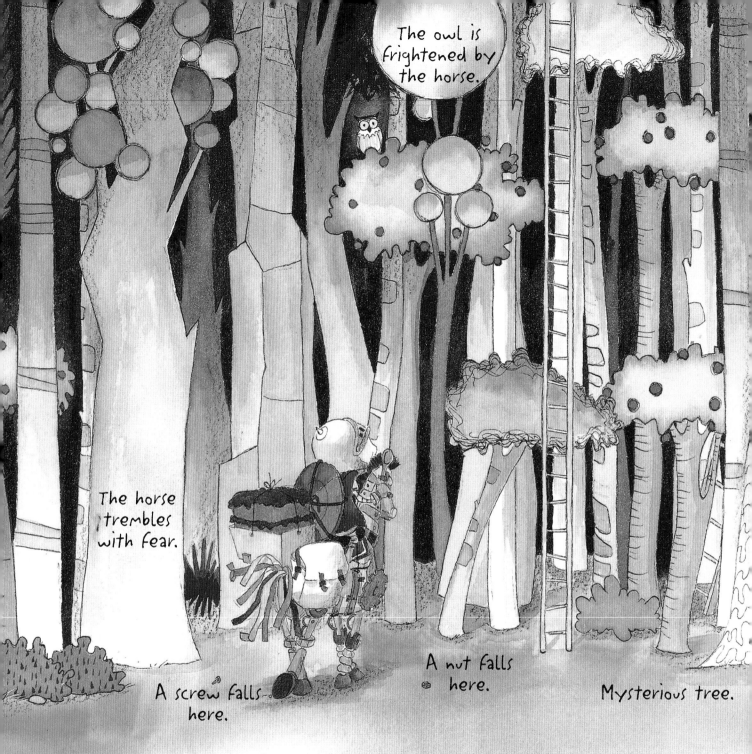

The little knight filled his satchel with huge pieces of chocolate cake. With the help of his friends, he put on his new equipment. He climbed on the old iron horse. Then, facing his destiny, he headed into the forest.

A very friendly bat.

A terrible monster hides in this tree trunk.

The groundhog is frightened by the horse.

Each time the sky lit up, the old horse shook and tried to turn around. Each time, the little knight whispered kind words and fed it huge pieces of chocolate cake to calm it down.

Deep in the heart of the forest, the smell of smoke was in the air. But it was only some loggers celebrating around a huge campfire.

A bit farther along, it was just a witch
fanning the flames under her big
cauldron.

The little knight continued on his path through the dark and the fog. Owls were flying everywhere. The old horse was shaking with fear. Each time its teeth chattered — CLICK! CLICK! CLACK! — a piece of metal fell onto the ground. BING! BANG! BANG!

A very solid metal pin.

A piece of pipe.

A large piece of metal.

PING! OUCH! A nut falls
on the hare's head.

Pretty bow.

A big pair of pliers.

Each time, with pliers and screws,
the little knight repaired the
horse's mane, face, hooves and tail.
Then he offered the horse a big
piece of cake.

After stopping to repair the horse more than ten times, the little knight finally arrived at the other end of the forest. The earth trembled. BOOOM! BOOOM! BOOOOOOOOM! The sky lit up. SWISHHHH!

A dragon emerged from the fire. Her mouth wide open, she growled and shot flames so strong that they reached up to the moon.

The little knight is brave but very frightened.

Flames as hot as an oven.

A very long dragon tail.

With one final chatter of its teeth, the horse broke into a thousand pieces. CLICK! CLICK! CLACK! BING! BANG! BANG!

The little knight found himself standing in front of a pile of scrap metal. He was also standing, all alone, in front of the terrible dragon.

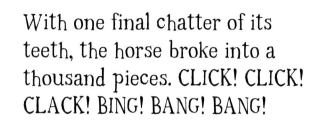

A useless piece of pipe.

His red cheeks show how hot he is.

The sword has become very hot.

The metal shield has become very hot.

A squirrel roasts a marshmallow.

Armed with his metal sword, the little knight approached the dragon. He worked his way toward her — closer, closer, closer — knowing that he could be devoured at any moment.

When he climbed up on a rock, he realized something: the dragon's foot was stuck in a trap and she was in a lot of pain.

A horrible trap.

A very sore leg.

This flame is so hot it may set the book on fire.

Even the
flowers are
amazed.

The little knight made a plan. Safely
behind his flame-proof shield, he threw
out insults at the dragon.

The dragon, getting angrier and angrier,
blew flame after flame after flame at the
little knight, until she almost fell over
from exhaustion.

New world
record for the
longest flame.

Then the little knight ran around the
dragon, faster and faster, until she
became so dizzy that she collapsed
to the ground.

The raccoon doesn't
believe its eyes.

The little knight
is exhausted but
happy.

Sore foot.

A bandage of ferns.

The little knight sprang into action. He used a scrap of metal to pry open the trap and free the dragon. Then, whistling a little song, he wrapped soft ferns around the dragon's injured foot to bandage it.

When the dragon woke up, she saw that the little knight had saved her life. With a giant tongue that smelled like fire, she licked the little knight's cheek. Then the dragon peacefully watched as her new friend rebuilt his horse from the pieces of metal, pins, nuts, bolts and slightly charred chunks of wood.

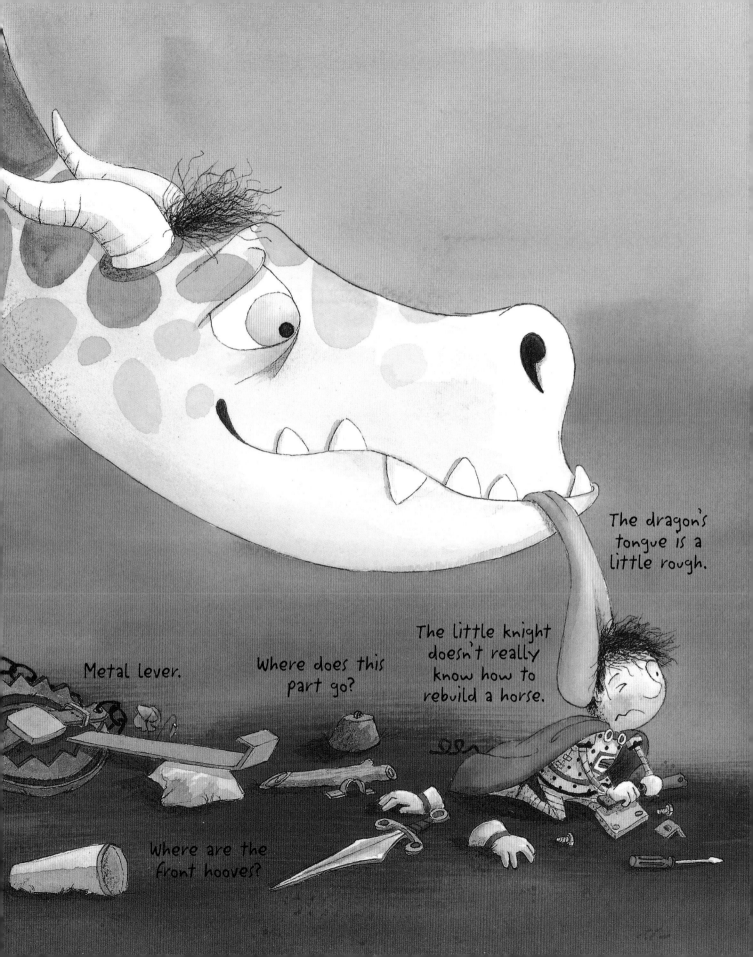

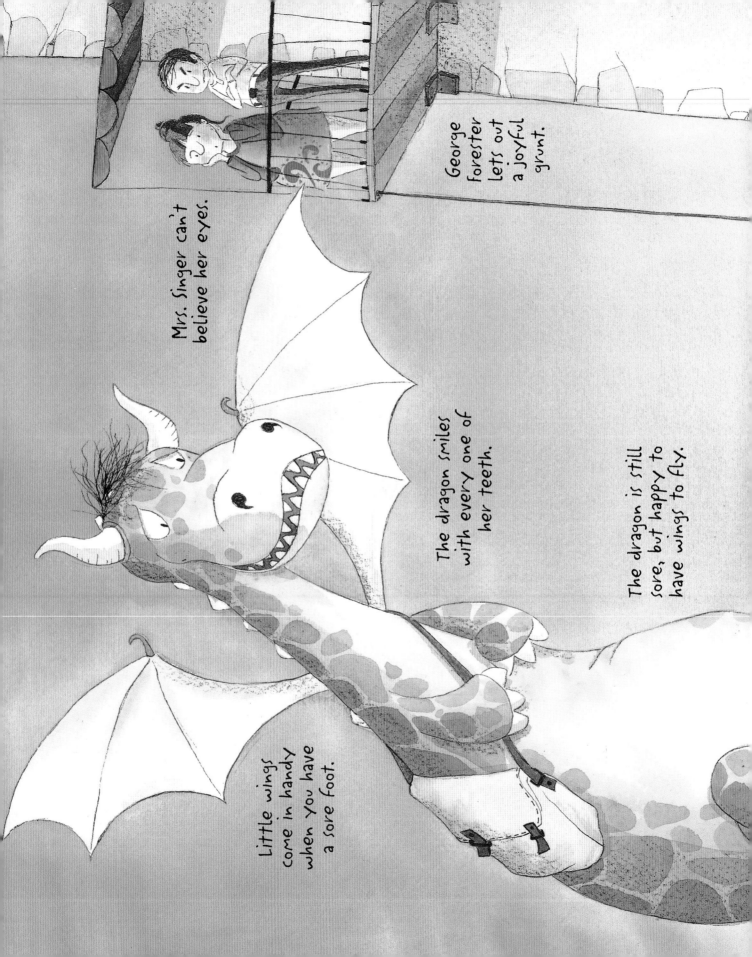

Mrs. Singer can't believe her eyes.

George Forester lets out a joyful grunt.

The dragon smiles with every one of her teeth.

The dragon is still sore, but happy to have wings to fly.

Little wings come in handy when you have a sore foot.

Just before sunrise, the villagers hidden away in the castle heard the noise again: BOOOM! BOOOM! BOOOOOOOOM! Terrified, they ran to look out the windows. They couldn't believe their eyes. The little knight had returned, mounted on a strange horse and accompanied by a dragon!

"All is well! No need to be afraid!" cried the little knight.

The horse looks different but is stronger than ever.

The wheels squeak a little.

Bartlett is happy to see the little knight, but she's still very scared of the dragon.

Big bonfire.

The villagers gathered loads of wood for the fire, and gathered together around it. With a single breath, the dragon lit a huge bonfire, and everyone celebrated into the night. The little knight sang his own little song and danced his own little dance.

The little knight dances his dance.

The Singer triplets dance like crazy.

Bartlett tries to roast a marshmallow.

The moon is a little bit jealous.

The witch dances for the first time in her life!

The ogre dances for the first time in his life!

Finally, everyone fell asleep,
knowing that from now on, cold
nights would feel much warmer.